The Orphan Duck

Ecaterina Barnutz

PAGE PUBLISHING
Conneaut Lake, PA

First originally published by Page Publishing 2023

ISBN 979-8-88793-800-4 (pbk)
ISBN 979-8-88793-811-0 (digital)

Printed in the United States of America

Dedication: Dumitrescu Dumitru

Stories were a gift from my father, who showed me how to marvel at them. He introduced me to books full of magic and wonder, where I could lose myself in their amazing worlds. I would eagerly await his return from work, hoping for another story. Even when he was tired, he would always have time to give me a smile and read me a story. To this day, his stories still capture my heart, and I will always remember them for the rest of my life.

Once upon a time, there was a grumpy old eagle named Ben who started to lose his feathers and eyesight. He lived high in the mountains on a large tree surrounded by a dense forest. Although many animals lived in the woods, they all feared the eagle and stayed far away from his tree. When he was young, Ben was a giant eagle famous for his size, strength, speed, and short temper.

*****

One night, there was a terrible storm. The storm was so strong that the lightning could be seen and heard from many miles away, with such heavy rain that even the tightly shut shutters clattered with noise.

Ben was warming himself by the fire, drinking tea, and smoking his old pipe. He loved to be alone and not to be bothered by anybody. As Ben continued smoking his pipe, there was a soft knock on the door. Nothing but the wind, he thought. However, the knocking became louder and more persistent.

Who could be bothering me at this hour? he thought.

Slowly getting up from his chair, he began moving toward the door. When looking through the window, he saw no one. He opened the door to be sure, but still, no one was there.

Somebody is trying to play a joke on me, he thought.

Before he closed the door, he heard a slight sound. To his surprise, the sound came from a small basket in front of the door. In the basket lay a tiny baby duck. Ben pushed the basket away as the door slammed loudly behind him.

"It is not my problem," he said aloud.

The storm continued to get stronger. The rain was pouring down the windows, and the branches of the tree twisted and turned against the strong winds. The baby duck felt cold and hungry and started to cry. Ben was old, but his hearing was still excellent. He was unable to enjoy this warm fire with that crying. He decided to bring the tiny basket inside.

"Just for tonight, you can stay here. Just no more crying," the eagle said to the baby duck.

*****

Just before the door closed behind the eagle, a hawk walked in. It was his friend, his only friend. Every morning, his friend would come to take him to their daily hunt. Ben called him Big Feet because his feet were huge. Big Feet turned toward his friend and asked, "What is that small thing in the basket?"

"I do not know. Somebody left that baby at my door last night," Ben said with a concerned look.

"A baby?" Big Feet said in disbelief. "You cannot keep the baby. It's too much work and noise."

"You are right," Ben said in agreement with Big Feet. "I will leave the baby in the forest after the rain stops. Somebody will take the baby."

Ben turned and looked at the baby, who was still crying. He got a piece of a small worm, and the baby opened her beak and ate fast and with pleasure. "You are like me. You like to eat tasty worms." He smiled with satisfaction.

*****

Once the storm died, Ben the Eagle picked up the small basket and flew down to the forest. He looked around and found a nice quiet place to leave the baby duck. The eagle just started flying away until a thought hit him: *Should I see who will take the baby duck?*

When he returned, wolves surrounded the basket, hungry for fresh meat. They were ready to grab the baby duck without any hesitation.

At the top of his lungs, Ben yelled, "Don't you dare lay a finger on that duckling!"

The wolves feared the giant eagle, and they ran away terrified. He took the baby, and he returned home.

*****

"Do not worry, I will find you a loving home," Ben said to the duckling.

The little duck looked at him with innocent eyes and opened her small beak again, her small beak showing him she was hungry.

"You did not even realize those wolves wanted to eat you. You are like me, not scared and caring only for your stomach." He laughed hard.

He took another piece of worm and gave it to the baby. "Eat and grow strong like me."

The baby duck ate and, in a few moments, fell asleep. The old eagle covered the baby and looked with kindness in his eyes.

"Look at you! You look like a mother, soft, and only tears are missing," Ben heard an old voice behind him say. It was Big Feet.

"Do not joke with things like that!"

"What do you think your neighbors will say when they find out? The mighty eagle, the king of the sky, protects a baby duck! Everybody will laugh at you." Big feet said with a large grin on his face.

"I know, but do you have the heart to abandon this baby?"

Big Feet looked at the duck sleeping peacefully, and his heart started warming. "I know. Take these worms. I had too much food at home."

"Thank you."

*****

Day by day, the two friends helped each other to raise the little duck. Days passed, and the duck grew bigger and stronger.

However, one day the eagle heard a desperate cry. The little duck broke her wing trying to fly from the tree. All the animals were laughing and making rude jokes about the little duck.

"O little ugly girl, you are worthless, ugly orphan duck!"

The old eagle flew close and looked furiously at them, and everybody froze in fear.

"Stop laughing. This is my child."

He was old, but even now, they feared him. He looked at them with his fierce eyes, and they ran away. The little duck tried to move, but her wing was hurting bad. He helped the little duck fly back home.

When they returned to their house, he looked at her face and saw tears in her eyes. "What is wrong? Why are you crying?

"I am not crying out of pain or because they were making fun of me. I am crying because I am happy."

"Why are you happy?" Ben the Eagle wondered.

"I am happy you called me your daughter."

"Oh! It is nothing. You pay too much attention to insignificant things."

He was smiling, thinking how much a simple word could make her happy. They were eating quietly, and suddenly the door opened, and Big Feet the Hawk came with lots of delicious worms. "I heard the news."

"No!" the baby duck said. "I will try harder to be the best hunter like you, and nobody will laugh at me again."

"I am sure my child will be the best."

In his friend's eyes, the hawk saw tears. "What is that? Are you getting soft?"

"Of course not, you simply brought too much dust from the outside." The old eagle laughed loudly. "Do you know how I met this troublemaker?"

"No, tell me, father."

When Ben heard the word *father*, he coughed, trying to hide his emotions.

"One day, when I was young and powerful, I was flying and looking for something to hunt. I saw wolves trying to attack a hawk. He could not fly because he was hurt badly, but he fought heroically. Impressed by how stubborn he was, I flew near that place. Hurt and bleeding, with no chance to live, the hawk still never gave up. The wolves saw me and ran away. From that moment, we become good friends, hunting together and spending lots of time."

"It is a good story and a strong friendship."

*****

Every night, the small duck asked her father to tell her a story. Her father's tales made her happy and gave her the courage to believe in herself.

Time passed, and the little duck, who was now known as Steel, was getting bigger, stronger, and faster. She learned from her father how to fly and how to hunt. But the most important thing was that she learned not to be scared.

The little duck helped animals from the forest, and they called her the Protector. She would bring food for tiny babies and whistle to let them know she was back. The animals would run happily to see her. Her father was getting older; he flew less and spent more time near the fireplace.

One day, when Steel returned from her daily flying, she saw wolves attacking somebody. She flew in that direction to help. She did not realize it was her father; she left him at home, sleeping peacefully. Her heart started to beat faster, and she knew she could not save him by herself in a second. Steel was determined to fight the wolves even if she would die.

Her father saw her and screamed, "Go, fly away! Leave me please! Save your life, my sweet child!"

"No, I am not going to leave you!" Steel yelled loudly.

On her way to save her father, she whistled something like a desperate cry for help. Everybody from the forest, old and young, came to help her. She bravely stood between her father and the wolves, fighting them without fear of death. Even the wolves were amazed by her boldness, but they did not leave.

Steel the Duck and her father, Ben the Eagle, forced the wolves to hunt outside the forest for so long that they grew to hate them. The oldest wolf remembered how many times the eagle made him run away ashamed. Now he was in command of a pack of wolves and wanted to teach them both a lesson.

But animals from everywhere came to save Steel and Ben. Even the scared rabbits were attacking the wolves. All the animals in the forest united to protect the old eagle and the duck.

"Boss, they are too many! What are we supposed to do?" one wolf asked the old wolf.

"Do not run away. The animals cannot scare us."

"But they are so many, and we are just a few of us and scared."

"Stay strong. Do not back out!"

"We are leaving, boss!"

They ran away, and the old wolf followed them. He left mad and promising to be back.

The Steel the Duck and Ben the Eagle were happy and thankful to all the forest animals.

"See, father, together we are strong!"

"My child, I learned a good lesson today. Being alone without friends is not safe." Ben said smiling towards his daughter.

They lived happily ever after in that forest, in harmony and peacefully with their friends.

The End

About the Author

I was born in Romania and have lived in Illinois for most of my life. I was inspired to write my stories while working in hospitals for many years and seeing so much suffering and fighting between life and death. I graduated from Chamberlain University with a bachelor's degree in nursing and two more associates in science. I decided to write my stories to give back hope. Through my books, children can learn how amazing life can be. My message is simple: Never give up on your dreams because your life can be the next amazing book.